Goldilocks and the Three Bears

illustrated by Estelle Corke

Child's Play (International) Ltd
Swindon Auburn ME Sydney

Printed in China
ISBN 978-0-85953-608-0 (h/c) ISBN 978-1-904550-19-8 (s/c)
5 7 9 10 8 6
www.childs-play.com

Once upon a time, there were three bears,
who lived in a house in the middle of a wood.
The father was a great big bear.
The mother was a middle-sized sort of bear,
and their young child was very small and timid.

One beautiful morning, they made porridge for breakfast. While it was cooling, they decided to go for a walk.

While they were away from the house, a little girl came by. Her name was Goldilocks. She hadn't meant to go very far from her parents, but she had taken the wrong turn, and then another, and then another.

Now, she was lost in the wood. The sky grew dark and it started to rain. She might be lost forever!

Goldilocks carried on through the trees, when all of a sudden she saw the bears' house. It looked friendly and welcoming. "I can shelter here," she thought. "And maybe someone can tell me how to get out of the wood."

When she looked through the window, though, there was no-one at home, so she went in.

There was a delicious smell of porridge in the air, and Goldilocks was very hungry. She found three bowls on the table. She tried the biggest bowl first, but it was too hot, and she burned her tongue. She tried the middle-sized bowl, but that was too cold.

Last of all, she tried the smallest bowl,
and that was just right. Lovely!

"I'm so tired now," thought Goldilocks, "I need to sit down." She sat in the biggest chair, but it was much too hard. Then she sat down in the middle-sized chair, and that was too soft. So she sat on the smallest chair, and that was just right. Lovely!

But just as she was getting comfortable, the little chair broke, and she fell flat on the floor.

"I think I need a rest," thought Goldilocks, and she went upstairs. She tried the biggest bed, but it was hard and lumpy. Next, she tried the middle-sized bed, but that was much too soft.

So she lay down on the smallest bed, and that was just right. Lovely! And she fell fast asleep.

Meanwhile,
the three bears
had finished their walk.
Now they were hungry,
and all of them were
looking forward to their
porridge as they made
their way home.

Father Bear sat down first, and noticed that someone else had tried his breakfast.
"Someone's been eating my porridge!" he growled.
"Someone's been eating my porridge, too!" grumbled Mother Bear.

"And someone's been eating my baby porridge!" wailed Baby Bear. "And they've eaten it all up!"

"Let's sit down
and think who
it might be,"
said Father Bear.

"Wait a minute!"
"Someone's been
sitting in my chair!"

"Someone's been sitting
in my chair, too,"
grumbled Mother Bear.

“Someone’s been sitting in my baby chair,” wailed Baby Bear. “And they’ve broken it into little pieces!”

"Perhaps they're still in the house," said Mother Bear. "Let's look upstairs."

"Look at this," growled Father Bear. "Someone's been sleeping in my bed."
"And someone's been sleeping in my bed, too!" grumbled Mother Bear.

"Someone's been sleeping in my baby bed," wailed Baby Bear.
"And they're still in it!"
"Be careful!" warned Father Bear.
"They could be dangerous!"

All the growling woke Goldilocks from her dream. With a very loud and very long scream that terrified all three bears, she jumped out of bed, and ran down the stairs and through the front door.

n her fright, she ran straight home
without once getting lost, and was
ust in time for another breakfast.

The bears got on with their day.

Father Bear made them all another pot of porridge. Mother Bear mended Baby Bear's chair.

And they never left their front door unlocked again!